DISCARD

# Beetle Boy

Inspired by Franz Kafka's "The Metamorphosis"

Lawrence David ✳ illustrated by Delphine Durand

A Doubleday Book for Young Readers

A Doubleday Book for Young Readers
Published by

Bantam Doubleday Dell Publishing Group, Inc.
1540 Broadway
New York, New York 10036

Doubleday and the portrayal of an anchor with a dolphin are
trademarks of
Bantam Doubleday Dell Publishing Group, Inc.

Text copyright © 1999 by Lawrence David
Illustrations copyright © 1999 by Delphine Durand

All rights reserved. No part of this book may be reproduced or trans-
mitted in any form or by any means, electronic or mechanical, including
photocopying, recording, or by any information storage and retrieval
system, without the written permission of the Publisher,
except where permitted by law.

Library of Congress Cataloging-in-Publication Data

David, Lawrence.
Beetle boy / by Lawrence David ; inspired by Franz Kafka's
Metamorphosis.
p.    cm.
Summary: After Gregory Sampson wakes up one morning to discover
that he has become a giant beetle, only one person seems to notice.
ISBN 0-385-32549-5
[1. Beetles—Fiction.  2. Metamorphosis—Fiction.]  I. Title.
PZ7.D28232Be   1998
[E]—dc21                                                    97-18961
                                                               CIP
                                                               AC

The text of this book is set in 17-point Zemke Hand.
Book design by Ericka Meltzer O'Rourke

Manufactured in the United States of America
March 1999
10 9 8 7 6 5 4 3 2 1

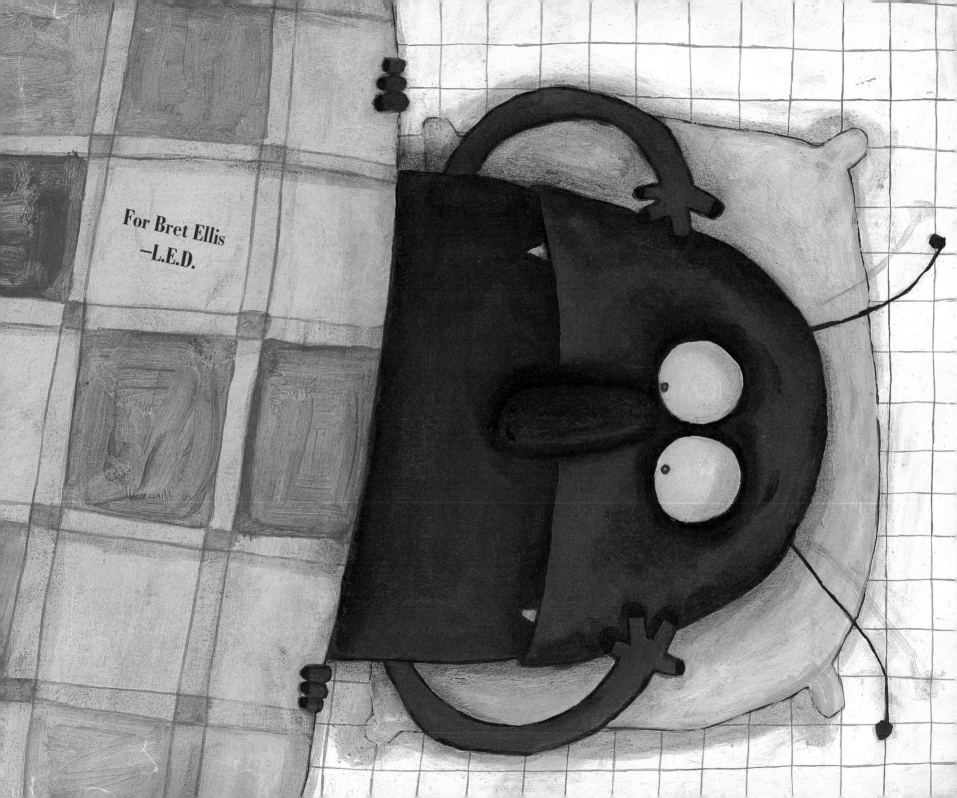

For Bret Ellis
—L.E.D.

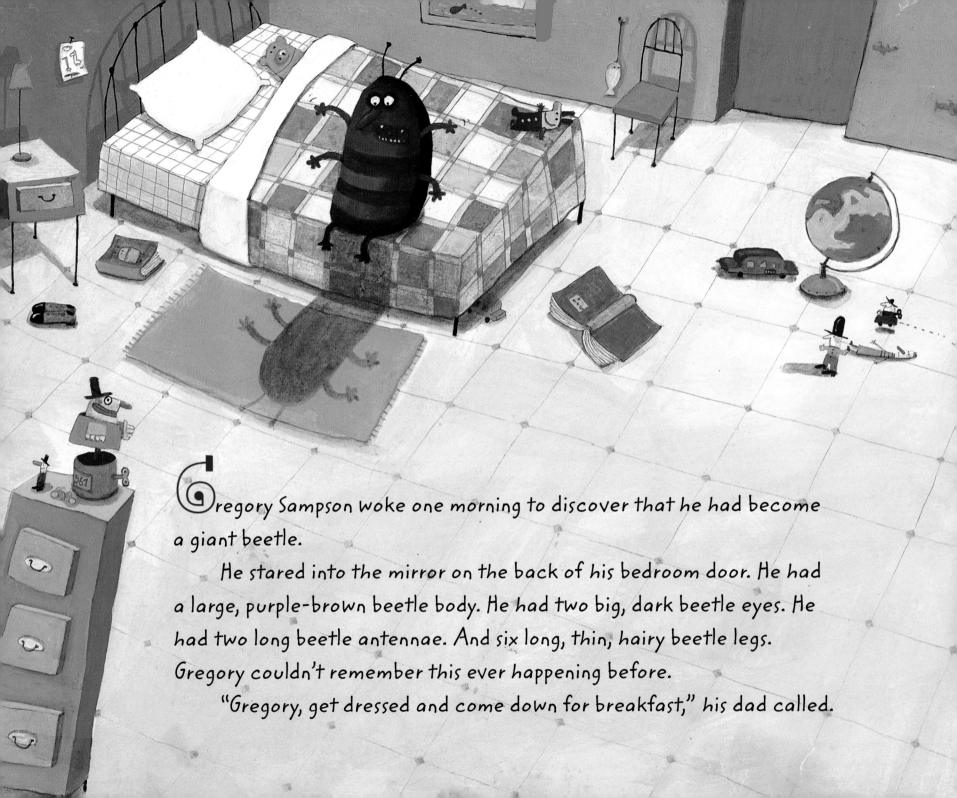

Gregory Sampson woke one morning to discover that he had become a giant beetle.

He stared into the mirror on the back of his bedroom door. He had a large, purple-brown beetle body. He had two big, dark beetle eyes. He had two long beetle antennae. And six long, thin, hairy beetle legs. Gregory couldn't remember this ever happening before.

"Gregory, get dressed and come down for breakfast," his dad called.

Gregory tossed himself down on all sixes and scurried into the bathroom. His beetle claws clicked against the floor tiles. Gregory washed himself and brushed the large, sharp fangs that protruded from his mouth. He looked in the mirror above the sink and scared himself. Yup, he was still a beetle.

Gregory had never seen a bug wearing clothes before, but most bugs didn't have to dress for a day at school. He rummaged through his dresser and took out a baggy shirt and pants with an elastic waistband. The pants weren't too much of a problem to pull on, but the shirt had only two armholes. Second-grade boys were not supposed to have six insect legs. Gregory cut two more holes in the shirt for his two new arms. Or were they legs?

"Gregory!" his mother yelled. "Hurry, please!"

Gregory scampered down the stairs a bit too fast, doing two back and three side flips along the way. He landed at the bottom on his beetle shell back. His six legs kicked at the air as he tried to right his body. Finally, after a few minutes of wriggling, he was able to grab hold of the banister and flip himself over so that his claws met the floor.

No one looked up as Gregory entered the kitchen. Dad stood at the counter packing school lunches for Gregory and his little sister, Caitlin. Mom sat at the table reading the newspaper. Caitlin was drinking a glass of orange juice. Her plate was piled with bread crusts and half an egg yolk.

Gregory hoisted himself into his chair and began eating his eggs and bacon. "Mom," he called, "Dad, Caitlin, I'm a bug. Look at me. I'm a giant beetle."

Dad closed the lunch boxes and smiled at Gregory. "And I'm a hippo."

Gregory waved a claw. "But I'm a bug, Dad, don't you see? What should we do?"

Mom answered from behind the paper. "You've always been our little bug-a-boo."

Caitlin wrinkled her nose. "Yesterday you said you wanted to be an astronaut." She picked a piece of bacon off Gregory's plate. "Do bugs like bacon?"

I am a bug

"Do you know how to change me back?" Gregory asked his mother. "Did this ever happen to you when you were a little boy?" he asked his father.

"Can't we discuss this after school?" Mom replied. "You have to get out to the bus."

Dad walked Caitlin and Gregory to the front door and handed them their lunches and backpacks.

"Can bugs be astronauts?" Gregory asked his father.

Dad laughed and gave his son a pat on his shell.

Gregory stared at himself in the hall mirror. Yup, still a bug. Couldn't anyone see?

Gregory and Caitlin strolled to the bus stop. Gregory found it was easier carrying his backpack and lunch box with four arms. When two got tired, he switched to the other pair. He offered to carry Caitlin's lunch box and backpack.

"How? You only have two hands, and they're already full," she lectured her older brother.

Gregory poked his sister with an antenna. "Can't you see I'm a bug?"

Caitlin ran off to play with her friends.

No one at the bus stop even noticed Gregory. Standing on the sidewalk, he looked down at the pavement. He carefully avoided stepping on any of the critters that ran around his legs. Were these his new brothers and sisters? Were his new mom and dad down there somewhere?

On the school bus, Gregory walked down the aisle and stood beside the seat where his best friend, Michael, sat. Michael saw Gregory's lunch box in the large beetle's claws. Michael saw Gregory's backpack hanging over the large beetle's thick shell. Tears formed in Michael's eyes. "What have you done to Gregory?" he asked in a whisper. "Where's my bestest friend?"

Gregory crept past Michael and sat in the window seat. "It's me," Gregory said quietly. "I woke up like this and no one cares. What can I do?"

Michael inspected his friend more closely. "How did it happen?"

"I don't know."

"Does it hurt?"

"No."

"Do you want to see a doctor? Get some medicine?
Maybe you should go to the school nurse."

"Do you think she's ever seen a second-grader who's a bug
before?" Gregory asked. "I don't think so."

Michael looked away from his beetle friend.
"No, but she once saw Monica Brawley
with a pen stuck up her nose.
That wasn't pretty."

The bus pulled up to the school. Kids ran down the bus steps, yelling and laughing and greeting their friends.

"Should we go in?" Michael asked. "Maybe during library we can look up what kind of beetle you are. Do you think that would help?"

"Maybe," Gregory replied. "I suppose I should know who I am if I'm going to be an insect."

The two friends walked into the schoolyard. No one looked at Gregory. No one paid any attention to the fact that he was a bug.

"Do you think I've always been a bug and no one ever noticed before and I only just noticed this morning?"

"I'd have noticed," Michael said.

"Are you sure?" Gregory asked.

In class, Ms. Dobson asked what two times three equaled.

"Six!" Gregory shouted.

"Come up and show your work on the blackboard," Ms. Dobson instructed.

Gregory drew an oval beetle body with six legs, three on each side. "Two sets of three makes six," he explained.

"Good job," Ms. Dobson said.

"No fair," Michael told his friend. "You counted on your legs."

In gym, they practiced dribbling the soccer ball and kicking at the net. Michael played goalie. Gregory raced down the field, flipped the ball from the ground to his shell, then gave it a strong *whap* with an antenna. The ball sailed through the air, over Michael's head, and into the net.

"Score!" Gregory yelled.

"No fair!" Michael exclaimed. "No one said you could use your antenna!"

During the last class of the day, Ms. Dobson took all the kids to the library.

Gregory chose the *Encyclopaedia Britannica*, Volume B for Bugs. Michael chose a book about insects. The friends sat at a table and began paging through the pictures.

"I never knew there were so many kinds of bugs," Gregory said.

"I'm glad you're the only big bug," Michael replied. "Just imagine if all bugs were as big as you."

Then Michael pushed his book in front of Gregory. "Wait, look here!" Michael shouted.

"Shhh," said the librarian.

"What?" Gregory asked.

Michael pointed. On page six was a large illustration that looked like a portrait of Gregory, only without a shirt and pants.

"'*Carabus problematicus,*'" Gregory read. "'Or ground beetle.'" He licked a claw, then stroked an antenna. "Hmmm . . ."

"What do you think?" Michael asked.

Gregory laughed. "It's kind of fun seeing my picture and name. Can I take it out?"

"Sure," Michael replied. "I found it for you."

"Time to go, class," Ms. Dobson announced.

Gregory held the picture of himself up to his teacher.

Ms. Dobson wrinkled her face. "Ugh, a bug!" she rhymed.

"Do you think it looks like me?" he asked.

Ms. Dobson laughed. "I never knew you to be such a silly boy," she answered.

The two friends rode the school bus home. No one mentioned to Gregory that he had become a beetle. Not the bus driver. Not the lunch lady. Not his teacher. Not one of the other kids. Not even his parents or sister. Only Michael.

"What does it mean that no one sees I'm a ground beetle?" Gregory asked. "Doesn't it matter whether I'm a little boy or a beetle? Doesn't anyone care?"

"I care," Michael said. "It matters to me. I think people should be people and beetles should be beetles. Not beetles people and people beetles. That's the way things are supposed to be." He shook his head. "I don't know why you've done this to yourself."

"I don't either," Gregory replied sadly.

"Do you know how to change back?" Michael asked.

"No. I mean, it's not so bad being a beetle, but I didn't want to be."

At the bus stop, Caitlin pointed at her brother. "He thinks he's a bug," she told her best friend. The two girls laughed and ran off to play.

Gregory arrived home. Mom was cutting carrots for a salad while she talked on the phone. She waved hello to Gregory.

"Mom," Gregory called. "I'm still a beetle."

"Okay, honey, have fun." She took a bite of a carrot.

Gregory went up to his room and shut the door. He felt like crying, but instead crawled up the wall and across the ceiling. He hung there and stared down at his bedroom below.

Hours passed.

He watched the sun setting upside down through his bedroom window. It looked as if it was rising.

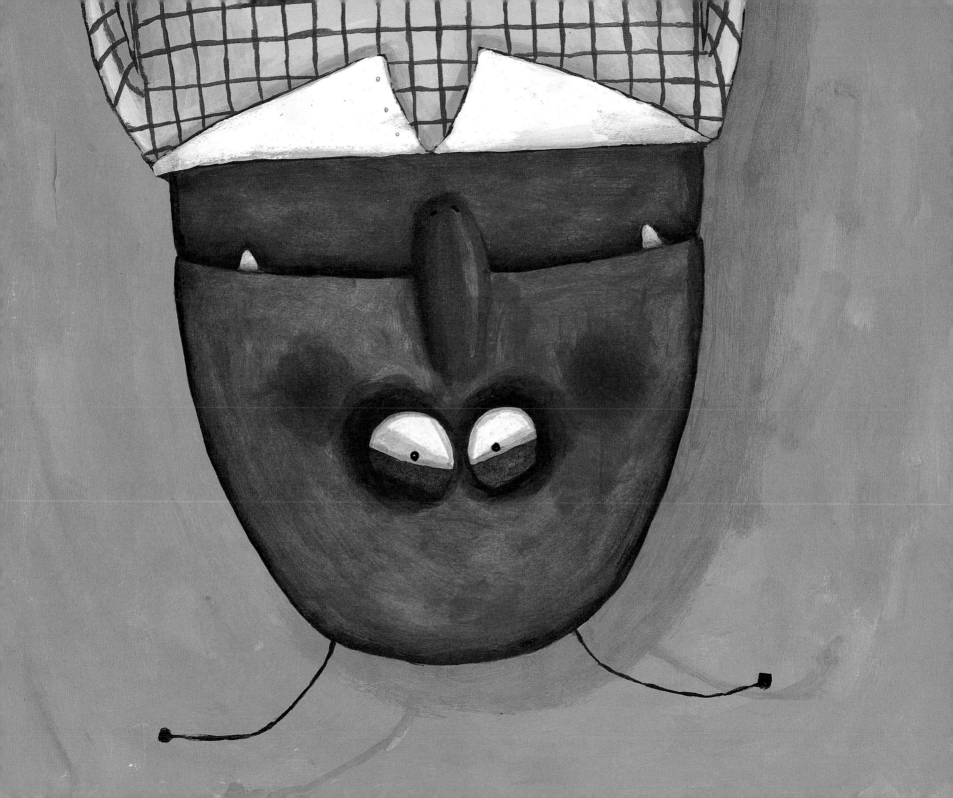

"Gregory, dinner!" his father called.

Gregory would not come down from the ceiling.

"Gregory, dinner!" his mother shouted.

Gregory would not come down from the ceiling.

There was a knock at the bedroom door.

"Come in," Gregory said.

Gregory's dad entered. "Dinner's ready. Where are you? I'm not playing games," he said in a stern voice.

"I'm up here," Gregory called.

Dad looked up and saw a large purple-brown beetle peering down at him. "Gregory?" he asked. "Is that a costume?"

"No, it's me. I'm a bug. I've been a bug all day and no one even noticed, except for Michael."

Gregory's mom and Caitlin came into the room. "Is something wrong?" Mom asked.

"Where's Gregory?" Caitlin asked.

Dad pointed to the ceiling, and Gregory's family all looked. No one said a word. No one could think of a thing to say. Gregory simply hung from above like a chandelier.

"I never wanted to be a bug," Gregory explained. "It just happened this morning, and then . . ." He began to cry. Large beetle tears splashed on the floor.

"Come down here," Mom said.

"Please," Dad said.

"Will you hurt me?" Gregory asked. "Will you spray me like you do the bugs in the backyard?"

"Of course not," Dad said.

"Of course not," Mom said.

"Will you sting us?" Caitlin asked.

Gregory waved his antennae at his sister. "No, I don't even have a stinger. And I wouldn't sting you if I did."

"Come down, dear," Mom said.

Gregory slowly crawled across the ceiling and down to the floor.

His family gave him a hug. His mom and dad kissed his beetle head. Caitlin refused. "I'm too young to be kissing bugs," she said. "And my lips are chapped."

"That's okay," Gregory replied.

"I'm sorry we didn't notice before," Dad said.

"I'm sorry I didn't listen," Mom said.

"What's it like being a bug?" Caitlin asked. "Can you be my show-and-tell?"

Gregory crawled into his bed and pulled up the covers with his six arms and legs. "I'm going to sleep. I've been hanging on that ceiling all afternoon and I'm exhausted. It's not as easy being a beetle as you might think."

Mom and Dad each gave him a kiss goodnight.

"Do you still love me now that I'm a beetle?" Gregory asked.

"We'll always love you," Dad replied.

"Be you boy or bug," his mother added.

Gregory's family left the bedroom, and Gregory quickly fell into a deep sleep.

Gregory Sampson awoke the next morning to discover he was no longer a bug. He stretched his arms and legs and climbed out of bed. He dressed and stood before the mirror on the back of his bedroom door.

"Nope, not a beetle."

Gregory smiled. He knew his family would be happy he was a boy again.

And *he* knew Michael would be, too.

Gregory let up the shade and watched as an insect crawled across the outside of the windowpane. "You should have come by yesterday," he told the small critter. "Then I could have played with you." Gregory whooped with laughter and jumped high in the air. "Hurrah!" he shouted. He ran downstairs to show his little-boy self to his family.

Gregory Sampson's beetle day was done.

SANDY SPRINGS

OCT 1 4 1999

R0089021902

J
PICTURE DISCARD David, Lawrence
Beetle boy
DAVID R0089021902

18 SANDY SPRINGS
Atlanta-Fulton Public Library